Listen and follow...

1. Scan the QR code using the camera on your phone or tablet. (You might need to download a QR reader first.)

2. Click on the link that pops up.

3. Press play to hear the story being read aloud.

4. Turn the page when you hear the twinkle!

First published 2022 © Twinkl Ltd of Wards Exchange, 197 Ecclesall Road, Sheffield S11 8HW

ISBN: 978-1-914331-43-5

FSC
www.fsc.org
MIX
Paper from responsible sources
FSC® C022913

We're passionate about giving our children a sustainable future, which is why this book is made from Forest Stewardship Council® certified paper. Learn how our Twinkl Green policy gives the planet a helping hand at www.twinkl.com/twinkl-green.

Printed in the United Kingdom.

10 9 8 7 6 5 4 3 2 1

A catalogue record for this book is available from the British Library.

Twinkl is a registered trademark of Twinkl Ltd.

This Twinkl Originals book belongs to:

_____

_____

A Twinkl Original

Bug's Big Trip

Twinkl Educational Publishing

...but it's a long way **across** the plain to the pool.

'No one will notice if I hitch a lift,' thinks Bug.

So, he hides **behind** a leaf and waits.

He jumps **off** the branch and travels **up** Giraffe's neck...

...**under** Crane's wing...

...*in* Lion's mane...

...and **between** Zebra's ears.

Bug bounces **off** and lands **on** the ground.

He is nearly there!

But there are too many animals **in front of** him.
He can't see the water.

'I'm just in time,' thinks Bug. 'This thirsty lot have nearly drunk all the water!'

He gets ready to jump **into** the pool for a lovely wash...

...but Hippo gets there first!

'No bath for me today,' thinks Bug.
'I guess I'll just have a shower instead!'

Welcome to the world of Twinkl Originals!

Buy extra copies of Originals stories in our online shop!

Board books

Picture books

Longer stories

Books delivered to your door

Enjoy original works of fiction in beautiful printed form, delivered to you each half term and yours to keep!

1 Join the club at twinkl.com/book-club.

2 Enter your delivery address and choose your book type.

3 Enjoy a brand new book, every half term!

The Twinkl Originals app

Now, you can read Twinkl Originals stories on the move! Enjoy a broad library of Twinkl Originals eBooks, fully accessible offline.

Search 'Twinkl Originals' in the App Store or on Google Play.